I0722994

SPACE JUNK

Beginning no End

ANDREW BIXLER

PTP

Published by Pants Team Press.

Special thanks to Meghan Lear for editing these words and to Gary Bixler for providing the interior illustration.

For more information about this book and to receive updates on new releases, visit andrewbixler.com

ISBN: 978-1-7370607-5-8

Books by Andrew Bixler

Space Junk: Beginning no End

Space Junk

More Space Junk

The Deaths of Adam Jones
(Space Junk Book 3)

Pants Team Pink: Shameless Promotional Adventure
(Space Junk Book 4)

Author's Note

The story you are about to read is a prequel of sorts, but it was intended to provide a different experience depending on whether it is read before, during, or after the series comes to its eventual conclusion. I wanted it to serve as both an introduction to the universe as well as a kind of artifact capable of shedding new light on the events of the broader story as they unfold. I hope you enjoy this little detour as much as I have.

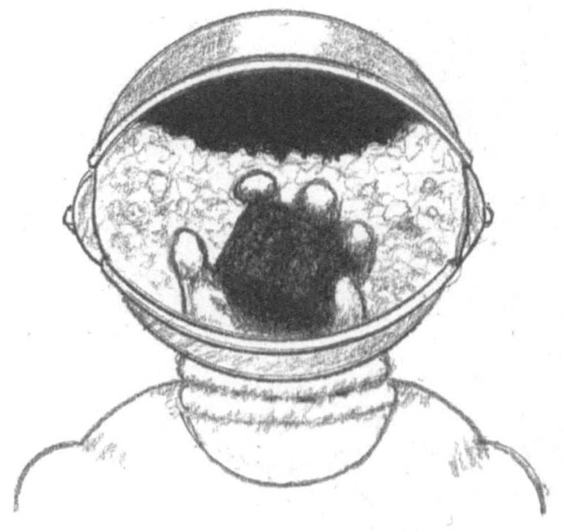

Beginning no End

Before his commanding trainee can wrench open the drop pod door, Blurp says, "Hold on a space second, will yuh! Are you sure we've exhausted all possible ways of getting out of this?"

Angrily shrugging Blurp's arm away, Whack-eth mouths something inside her battered academy-issued helmet, and a few space seconds later, her voice comes out over the static-laced communication channel, *Do you think I'd be here otherwise?*" The older girl, her sharp brow furrowing purposefully underneath her perfectly cropped golden hair, yanks the pod door handle back and the antique metal rod is torn from her fingers as the door is thrown open by the violent dust storm whipping across the moon's surface.

For a long moment, Blurp stares into the forbidding space-hellscape with thoughts of abdication dancing in his head, until Whack-eth finally shoves him out into the swirling gray dust. He immediately gets the sensation of being inside a holo-tube with bad reception, the particles of lunar soil and loose trash pelting his helmet with white noise as he desperately wills the image to come into focus.

Fighting the lunar wind, Whack-eth secures the pod door and points one arm of her bulky spacesuit in the direction of their objective, as indicated by a crude map displayed inside their portholes.

As they march across the ancient scrap dunes, Blurp begins to reconsider his whole career trajectory. When he first signed up to join the defenders of the most powerful organization of planets ever aligned, he imagined he'd be one of the elite, enjoying all the freedoms, fancy rations, and exclusive coupons that the application implied. Instead, he's out here wading through the trash like a common scrapper. It's elite trash, granted.

"Why are we out here, anyway?" he asks his 'space pal,' a term drilled into them while marching the gray grounds of the academy.

In a few moments, Whack-eth's voice scolds, *"You mean, you didn't read the brief?"* She groans impatiently before explaining, *"We've been sent to Garbo 112-B to investigate a particularly uninteresting anomaly reported over two hundred space years ago by the leading cosmologists of the time, which is to say that you know more about the universe than they did. By studying the movement of trash along gravitational currents, they hoped to discover why this particular moon became home to the densest garbage patch in the universe."*

"Sounds like a colossal *waste* of time," Blurp cleverly decides.

"What they claim to have discov—" Whack-eth continues but is presumably cut off by Blurp's belated comment. *"Funny, you're not far off. They never came to a consensus about the garbage patch, but their report indicates something even more dubious than their collective mental state. Long after they had all retired from their posts, they would*

still get together occasionally, taking advantage of their access to the UE's vast trove of surveillance data to calculate the mass of all the matter in the universe. You know, for fun. Before long, they noticed that the answer was gradually, ever so slightly, increasing. They repeated the calculations space year after space year, but the number continued to fluctuate just enough to measure. We're talking a fraction of a fraction of a raleigh. One of them finally suggested they were experiencing some sort of group hallucination, and the rest were inclined to agree, if only because it solved their problem."

"Is this going somewhere?" Blurp interjects, tripping over a pile of old space porno mags as he strains to keep sight of his space pal through the whirling sand.

"Now, after two centuries, some dumbskull had to go and prove the old fish heads right. Whoever dredged this report out of the mission backlog managed to roughly pinpoint the supposed source of the anomaly. And so, we're out here wading through the biggest trash heap in the universe, during the worst junk storm in recorded history, looking for evidence of Space God knows what, all because a couple ancient nerds stuck their sniffers someplace they didn't belong. Neither do anyone else's for that matter — I can smell the stench through my spacesuit."

"Okay," Blurp says, grappling to find his place in all of this. "But I meant, why are *we* out here instead of some other ackles?"

"You," Whack-eth says, pointedly, *"are here because you're so low on the chain of command that I could legally kill you right now and be commended for my superior decision-making. This is a job of least importance, hence... As to why you were chosen over the other equally worthless seamen, you must have done something especially stupid."*

"I did put bleach in the community shampoo bottle," Blurp laments. "Plus, there was that time the bunk got infested with moon mites from all the old ration trays under my bed. And last space month, I used the administrator account on the commandant's computer to change everyone's marks – I had him thinking he was unfit for duty until he noticed I was suddenly at the top of the class. Maybe it was one of those things. Anyway, I get it. I'm less than the scum that gets eaten by the other scum. But how did *you* wind up here?"

Whack-eth stops amidst the storming junkpile and glances back. *"I volunteered for this duty for the very same reason that it was foisted upon you. I'm setting an example. When they see that I'm willing to go on a mission this dangerous and chidiotic, they'll know I'm capable of anything."*

"O-kay," Blurp says. "But who's *they*?"

Ignoring the question, Whack-eth turns back and resumes trudging toward their sure-to-be-stupid, unquestionably fictional destination.

As Blurp stumbles after his prickly partner's dark silhouette, he figures he might as well kill two dust goblins with one swipe of his safety-sabre. So, he unzips his backsack and rummages around until he finds the handheld box he's been lugging around with him since he was a kid. Lately, its only function has been to act as a reminder of home. But every once in a while, he still gets to put it to its intended use.

With a yank of the antenna and a turn of the dial, the box's blurry monochrome screen gradually comes to life, and as Blurp waves the detector out in front of him, he's suddenly transported back to the craggy backyard on Zorma Inferus, searching the lifeless landscape for a treasure that isn't there.

"What the fish is that thing?" Whack-eth asks, glancing back through the curtain of dust.

"Well… it's…" Blurp stammers.

But before he gets a chance to concoct a plausible lie, Whack-eth asks, *"Is that a* black gold detector? *Ha! I haven't seen one of those since I was a kid. But why would you—"* Before she can finish the question, a strange combination of understanding, confusion, and pity crosses the hardened face behind the dusty porthole. *"You don't think you're going to find the black gold out here, do you?"*

"You never know," Blurp mumbles.

Laughing contemptuously, Whack-eth says, *"Correction, I always know. Now, put that thing away, before someone sees you and puts us away."*

"Who's going to see us out here?"

Gazing off for a moment, Whack-eth finally says, *"You got me there. Where'd you get it, anyway?"*

"Made it myself," Blurp says, proudly. "I sent away for the plans from an ad in the back of an old *Ghoul and The Gang* magazine when I was nine space years old. By the time I was twelve, I could almost read them."

Whack-eth scoffs, but as they slog through a sea of empty mood drink bottles and beer cans, she keeps glancing back at the machine, until she finally asks, *"So, is it working?"*

"I assume so…"

"You mean, you don't even know if it's doing what it's supposed to do?"

"Er, well, as a matter of fact," Blurp fumbles. "No."

"I misjudged you," Whack-eth says. *"If you think you're going to find any treasure on this chitball, you're even more clueless than I thought."*

But Blurp remains unswayed. "Sometimes the only thing keeping me going is the delusion that I could strike black gold. But I suppose you wouldn't understand that."

"You might be surprised," Whack-eth says, once she's done laughing. *"Hey, there it is."*

"Very funny," Blurp says. "You found the black gold. Even if I actually believed you, the detector isn't going off."

"I'm not talking about the black gold, you dumbcompoop," Whack-eth says, pointing toward a mountain of trash up ahead. *"We're almost at the location of the anomaly. Once we get there, we can make our report and head back to the pod."*

"But what if we don't find anything?" Blurp asks as he stuffs the detector back into his bag.

"Our orders aren't to find anything," Whack-eth says. *"No one has any expectation of discovering anything of any importance whatsoever."*

"You mean this has all been a big waste of time?" Blurp gripes.

"That's what I've been telling you."

When they finally reach the base of the great trash heap and Blurp gazes up at the rotting monument to universal waste, he suddenly feels an existential crisis coming on. The rubbish pile is so massive that, from his vantage, it looks as if the peak rises to the very edge of the moon's thin atmosphere and beyond.

Taking out her space pad, Whack-eth briefly glances up at the garbage pile, jots something down using the attached stylus, and concludes, *"Welp, that's that. We better hurry and get out of here before we get caught in this storm."*

"That's that?" Blurp cries. "I can't believe they sent us all the way out to this trash heap just to have a quick look around. As soon as we get back, the commandant is going to find his ack stuck to the toilet seat. And that's not one of those things that means something else." Whack-eth abruptly jumps back, shouting something and waving her hands, but before Blurp can hear her protests, he says, "You can stop defending them. I don't give a chit what excuse they—"

When her words finally reach Blurp's helmet, they come in loud and crackly, but clear. *"Fishing… RUN!"*

Following Whack-eth's finger, Blurp whips his head up to find a torrent of trash tumbling down the dark sky, and he knows that this is the end.

Blurp braces for a painful death, but it doesn't come as quickly as he thought it would, giving him just enough time to whimper as the colorful refuse hurtles toward him. But before he is unceremoniously returned to the junk pile from whence he came, a greater power intervenes to yank him out of harm's way.

He looks over his shoulder to find Whack-eth dragging him to safety as the trash gradually crashes to the moon's surface.

"What part of 'run' sounded like 'cower' to you?" Whack-eth inquires.

"It's like it fell in slow motion," Blurp says as gray moon dust plumes up around the man-made meteorites.

"You must have noticed the gravity here is only around half USG."

But Blurp just stares up at her, waiting for the words to make sense.

"Universal Standard Gravity," Whack-eth moans.

"Oh… right."

"Come on," she orders, wrenching Blurp to his feet. *"We have to find shelter before the storm picks up."*

Small bits of scrap begin raining down on them as they plod along the edge of the great trash mound, and soon they're being battered by a torrent of unidentified falling junk. Amidst the downpour, Blurp's foot slips on an old beer can, and he stumbles forward into a pile of garbage, which judging by the expiration date on the moon-nog carton pressed against his porthole, is older than he is.

"Don't you even know how to walk?" Whack-eth moans, turning back.

But as she lifts Blurp out of the scrap, he spots something unusual amidst the hail of trash and takes off ambling after it before Whack-eth has a chance to complain. Out in the open junkscape, the trash rains down freely, forcing him to dodge and weave for his life as, somewhere behind him, a hunk of junk lands with such force that it causes the lunar surface to quake. Doing his best to avoid the falling scrap, he races to the neon green puffball sticking out of the dust and gets to work digging it free. Once he can get his space gloves around it, he gives it a strong tug and it comes loose.

"What the fish are you doing?" Whack-eth shouts as she emerges from the dust.

Proudly holding onto his plushy prize, Blurp says, "It's an old Moon Maggot. I can't believe someone would throw this out."

"You're going to get us killed for some toy."

"I can think of a lot worse reasons," Blurp says as his space pal drags him back across the moon's littered surface.

"Over there!" Whack-eth motions to a dark hollow in the great trash heap where they can wait out the storm.

Evading potentially deadly debris all along the way, they reach the opening to find a large cave carved into the heap, its irregular arch supported by generation upon generation of compacted trash. Once they're in the safety of the junk hole, they gaze out at the raging storm trashing the moon's rocky surface, and as Blurp watches the bright objects float down through the sky, he can't help thinking it looks beautiful, in a purely artificial, baldly commercial sort of way.

"I guess we're going to be stuck here for a while," Whack-eth laments.

"At least I have my Moon Maggot," Blurp says, dusting off his vintage toy.

"Give me that!" Whack-eth grumbles, angrily snatching the bug-eyed stuffed animal out of Blurp's gloved fingers.

"Be careful!" Blurp cries. "Those things are rare. I bet it's worth a few hundred crits."

Shrugging dismissively, Whack-eth tosses the Maggot into the cave and says, *"It's space junk to me."*

Blurp tries to snatch the Maggot out of the thin atmosphere, but it slips through his fingers and lands in the dust. For a brief moment, he's outraged by Whack-eth's blatant disregard for the toy's condition. But his anger swiftly morphs into delight when, upon hitting the ground, the Maggot's head starts to emit a bright yellow glow.

"I don't believe it,' Blurp says, shuffling to collect his prize. "It still lights up! They don't make 'em like they used to, huh?"

Whack-eth rolls her eyes and turns her glare back toward the storm, as if wishing hard enough might force the trash to stop.

"If this Moon Maggot could survive these conditions, I wonder what other treasures are hiding out there," Blurp says.

Scrunching her nose like she just got a whiff of their current surroundings, Whack-eth snaps, *"This isn't a treasure hunt. You're training to become a member of the mighty Zorman fleet and, by extension, a citizen of the United Empires. Act like it, for Space*

God's sake. If you want to look for buried treasure, go waste your time drifting through space with the rest of the scrappers."

"Hey, what's that?" Blurp croaks as he spots something shiny further back inside the cave. Guided by his glowing Maggot, he retrieves a small rectangle of thin cardboard from the dust and carefully wipes it off on his spacesuit. "It's one of those Chibi-Sitcom cards – Half-Pint Hal, with special ability, 'Skip Work.' I wish I used that move today."

While Whack-eth impatiently waits for the storm to stop, Blurp examines the cave walls, searching for insight into the distant past. Afraid at first of what he might find, he soon discovers that beneath the extinct brand names and outdated packaging, his ancestors' trash wasn't so different from his own. But as he scans the crumpled and faded wrappers, he notices a startling phenomenon. He frantically checks the other packages, but they're all the same. Suddenly realizing that he's stumbled upon a terrible secret with repercussions stretching across the UE and beyond, he involuntarily gasps.

"What are you doing back there?" Whack-eth demands. *"The trash is going to quit any space second, I hope."*

"Don't freak out," Blurp says. "But I've discovered a plot so devious and lucrative that just saying it out loud may put our very lives in danger."

"You don't say…"

"Get this. Stuff used to cost *less* than it does now." When the information fails to elicit any reaction at all from Whack-eth, Blurp clarifies, "Like, *a lot* less."

"Not only that, but the rations used to taste better," Whack-eth deadpans.

"You noticed that too?"

"Why don't you do something useful," she suggests, *"like shuddup."*

Blurp swipes the words out of the dusty air, resolving to continue his amateur excavation even if he has to do it by himself. Using his Maggot to light the way, he stumbles into a world of scrap unlike anything he's ever seen. What at first glance looks like just another heap of trash is in fact a giant time capsule containing the history of the modern universe, or at least the discarded bits. The way the garbage is layered, he can actually make out the moment when the plastic figure epoch gave way to the first robo dynasty. Possibly even more incredible is the fact that he actually remembered something from his classes at the academy.

By the time he's completed a cursory dig, his bag is so packed with scrap that he's forced to carry most of his plunder back by hand. When Whack-eth lays eyes on the grubby bounty, her jaw drops so far that she can't seem to lift it back up.

"It's crazy what some people throw away," Blurp says, cheerfully.

When Whack-eth comes to her senses, she absently snatches a torn sex-bot flyer off the pile and says, *"What exactly are you planning to do with all of this? The commandant isn't going to let you bring this chit back to the academy. Plus, it'll exceed the drop pod's weight limit."*

"I'll rent a scrap freighter if I have to," Blurp says. "This place is a black gold mine."

Whack-eth closes her eyes, and when she opens them, she tells Blurp, *"I'm not going to get chewed out for going off-mission just because you want to bring back a bunch of ancient trash."*

"This isn't trash," Blurp argues. "It's treasure."

"There's a reason why it all ended up on this garbage ball in the first place," Whack-eth moans. *"Now, I'm going to give you about five space seconds to drag this chit back where it——"* But before she can

finish, something in the pile catches her eye, and she cautiously approaches to pull a soft artifact out of the junk.

"Isn't that brule?" Blurp says, pointing at the stuffed muscle-man puking green bile onto its chest. "It's a—"

"*Barf Buddy*," Whack-eth mutters reverentially. *"I used to have one just like this, a long time ago. I wonder where it came from."*

"I already told you, I got it from back there," Blurp scoffs, jutting his thumb at the dark tunnel behind them.

But as Blurp sorts through his haul, Whack-eth begins to look worried. *"No, I mean, this isn't regular trash. It's all semi-precious junk. How did it end up in here? And while we're at it, what caused this cave to be here?"*

But Blurp just shrugs. "We can't know for sure, but probably whatever that is."

Whack-eth's face turns ghostly pale, and she slowly turns to find an oversized set of beady eyes leering out of the darkness.

A lanky shadow skitters across the cave, and as Blurp makes a belated run for it, something wraps around his ankles and pulls his legs out from under him. Lifting his spinning head, he makes a futile attempt to free himself, when what looks like a gray glob of chewed-up bubble gum shoots out of the darkness and binds his wrists together with a thick, gooey substance. It all happens so fast that he doesn't even have time to grab his space gun.

"Shoot it!" Whack-eth cries as she wriggles in the dust, equally incapacitated.

"How the fish am I supposed to do that?" Blurp inquires. "What is that thing, anyway?"

"It must be a junk monster," Whack-eth says.

Frantically searching the dark as the creature prowls the edges of the cave, Blurp says, "You mean junk monsters are real? I thought they were just made up to scare kids away from playing on dump planets. What the fish are we going to do?"

Whack-eth's lack of solutions as she concentrates on freeing her hands does little to alleviate Blurp's fears. In trying to fill in the blank, his mind concocts a creature much worse than anything that could possibly exist – an all-powerful being with a body composed of gelatinous tentacles propping up the humorless, cyclopean face of the commandant. Mistaking Whack-eth's strained, staticky grunts for the monster's, Blurp fitfully kicks his legs out to squirm back along the cave floor.

"Good idea," Whack-eth says. *"If you free my hands, I can grab my space gun."* But as Blurp wiggles in the opposite direction, she shouts, *"Where are you going? That* thing *could be back any space second."*

In fact, Blurp can see the monster shifting in the shadows just beyond the pool of starlight spilling in through the mouth of the cave. "If I could just reach it…"

Something makes a loud *SWACK*, and Whack-eth frantically cries, *"Oh chit, oh chit, it's got me. Do something!"*

Pushing his way through his salvaged treasure, Blurp finally gets within nudging distance of his security toy and says, "As long as I have my Moon Maggot, everything will be all right."

"You stupid fish head!" Whack-eth screams.

"Yep, everything's going to be o-kay," Blurp says as he worms toward his Maggot.

Ignoring the horror taking place nearby, he sighs contentedly and lays his head on the grinning toy. When his helmet presses down on the Maggot's plush body, its molded head lights up, and a pained screech suddenly rings out through the cave. Trash crunches and clatters as the monster beats a hasty retreat back into the shadows, and with the darkness temporarily banished, the space pals are granted a few additional moments of precious life.

When Whack-eth recovers from the shock, she says, *"I owe you an apology. You knew the monster would be sensitive to light."*

"Uh, yeah, that's right!" Blurp says. "But no need to apologize for your ignorance, even if you should have known better."

"I never should have doubted you," she says. *"Although, you can understand why I did. You play the part of the know-nothing chidiot quite well."*

"Yeah, well, I've had a lot of practice," Blurp says. "Never mind that. What do we do now?"

"We've got to find a way out of here before that thing gets back," Whack-eth says as she tries to gnaw her way out of her binds. *"It's no use. What is this stuff, anyway?"*

Looking more closely at the viscous gunk holding his wrists together, Blurp reluctantly reports, "I think it's… spit."

"Ulch," Whack-eth groans, running her tongue across her teeth. *"As if I hadn't suffered enough indignity for one mission."* Pulling herself through the moon dust, she tells Blurp, *"Kick this way. We have to get loose."*

"How do we do that?" Blurp whines, helplessly.

When they get close enough to each other, they line up face-to-face, and Whack-eth instructs, *"Get my phone from my pocket and use the safety-saber to cut my hands free."*

Probing for the phone through the fat fingers of his spacesuit, Blurp says, "I think I got it."

But when he clumsily lifts the object, Whack-eth cries, *"Not the space gun! You'll shoot my hand off."*

Blurp carefully sets the gun down in the dust between them and tries again. This time he emerges with the proper piece of standard-issue hand-me-down hardware, and after a few space minutes fumbling to unlock it, he finally manages to equip the simple light knife. As he lays the blade across the thick gob of sputum, it begins to soften and then melt, until Whack-eth is able to pull her arms apart.

As soon as they dissolve the rest of the spit holding their appendages together, Whack-eth retreats toward the mouth of the cave, when Blurp calls, "Wait a space second. Don't you want to see what else that monster has stashed in here? If this is the kind of stuff it leaves lying out in the open dust, just imagine what it keeps back there."

Whack-eth's face twists as she stomps back to knock on her space pal's helmet. *"Hello, McBlurp! Are you completely out of your mind? That thing almost ate us for… whatever meal we'd be sitting down to right now if we hadn't gotten stuck on this stupid rock."*

"Snack time."

"Exactly."

"With the help of my Moon Maggot, not to mention our space guns, we'll be fine," Blurp argues. "And if that monster tries to attack us, we'll just do what we've been trained to do — explode the enemy. Anyway, didn't you say we're supposed to be investigating anomalies? I'd say this qualifies."

"This does technically fall within the purview of the mission," Whack-eth reluctantly concedes. *"And it would come as quite a shock to the commandant and the rest of the ackles at the academy to see*

us succeed at a hopeless task. For our purposes, the only thing better than finding nothing would be finding something."

"So, let's go!" Blurp says, holding out his Maggot to light the way. "I told you this thing was valuable."

Using his other hand, he draws his space gun and points it into the shadows as the two of them follow the trail of scrap down the dark tunnel. When a dust goblin suddenly jumps out from beneath a pile of old action figures, he reflexively fires, and the bright projectile illuminates a small portion of the long passageway before dissolving against the trash.

"What the fish!" Whack-eth shouts. *"Haven't you learned anything from your training? One wrong blast could bring this whole place down."*

"Don't you think I know that?" Blurp moans. "My finger slipped. These stupid gloves are too big."

"Gimme that," Whack-eth says, ripping the gun out of his hand. *"You obviously can't be trusted with it."*

As they cautiously continue down the corridor, something rustles the distant trash, and the gun goes off again.

"I told you," Blurp says.

"Did you see that?" Whack-eth asks.

"Oh sure, change the subject," Blurp grumbles, jutting his thumb out. "Or just admit that you're as scared as I am."

Pale-faced, Whack-eth lifts the gun and fires it down the tunnel. *"I think I saw something move."*

"Oh chit, it's the monster!"

"Don't panic!" Whack-eth commands. *"Like you said, as long as we stay in the light, it can't get us."*

While they await the monster's next move, the Moon Maggot's head starts flickering, and as if looking at a flame shuddering in the wind, they both hold their breath. Whack-eth points the gun in front of them as the sound of crunching trash grows closer, and they stare into the light behind the Maggot's bright eyes until it dims out.

With the afterimage of the Maggot's smiling face burnt into Blurp's retinas, the surrounding tunnel becomes blindingly dark. "Come on, you stupid thing," he negotiates with the toy as he throttles its plush body. "Light up!"

"Do you hear that?" Whack-eth says. *"It's coming for us."*

She fires the gun again, and in the brief moment that the cave is illuminated, Blurp spots a large gray shadow skittering along the wall.

Squeezing the stuffed Maggot to his chest, he tries a different tactic. "Please turn on. I promise, after this I'll take you home and give you all the fresh power cells you can drain. Just this one time, light up!"

Whether by fate, divine intervention, or good ol' fashioned dumb luck, the Moon Maggot manages to draw out some hidden reserve of power and flares back to life just in time to expose the monster standing in front of them.

A gray reptoid with a flat snout and large black eyes, its dry, scaly form towers over them like some sort of mythical trash demon. They all scream—the monster due to the light, Blurp and Whack-eth to extreme fear.

Whack-eth shoots Blurp's space gun wildly, but the few bolts of bright fire that manage to hit their target fail to do any damage.

"You chidiot!" Whack-eth shouts. *"You had it set to 'annoy.'"*

She fumbles with the power setting, but before she can get it switched to 'splode,' the monster opens its wide, dripping maw, and in one sick motion, it swallows the would-be officer of the mighty Zorman fleet and citizen of the United Empires whole.

Whack-eth goes down kicking and screaming, muffled as it is by the walls of the monster's esophagus. The thing doesn't even chew but rather tilts its head back and swallows, the girl's space boots flailing from its mouth as she slides down its wide gullet. The sight is nauseating, and Blurp turns away to keep from vomiting in his helmet.

When he looks back, Whack-eth is gone. In her place sits a giant bloated reptoid who, though full beyond capacity, stares at the young space cadet through hungry, bulging eyes. Blurp can see Whack-eth's hands pressing against the inside of the creature's swollen stomach, desperate to escape. But the monster seems less concerned with its prey than the light from the Moon Maggot. Shielding its eyes with its scaly paw, it attempts to drag itself back into the shadows, but its stomach is so full that it can barely move.

When Blurp finally breaks out of his fear-induced paralysis, he reaches for his space gun only to be reminded that Whack-eth took it with her into the bowels of the beast. Watching helplessly as the monster's stomach grows less agitated, Blurp worries that he's running out of time. If he returns to the academy without his space pal, he'll be dishonorably discharged, into deep space.

Unable to come up with a less horrific solution, Blurp pulls out his phone and engages the safety-saber. He grimaces at the thought of what he's about to do as he holds the saber out in front of him, aiming at the reptoid's distended gut, when the monster opens its maw and releases a loud belch. As the beast lunges forward, Blurp thrusts his saber at its stomach, and before either of them knows what hit them, the monster bursts apart in an explosion of unidentifiable viscera and black goo.

After a moment, Blurp wipes the gunk from his porthole and plods over to help Whack-eth out of a pool of monster blood.

When Whack-eth gets to her feet, she holds out a familiar-looking object covered in goop and says, *"You can have your space gun back."*

"Are you done fooling around now?" Blurp asks, carefully stuffing the weapon back in its holster.

Her face obscured behind a thick layer of black sludge, she sighs, *"Yes."*

Wiping off his Moon Maggot, Blurp lights the way as they continue down the dark tunnel. With the sounds of the storm battering the mountain of junk above them, they follow the trail of scrap until it seems as if they've gone far enough to come out the other end. Just as Blurp begins to wonder if they missed a turn somewhere, the path opens up, and they find themselves stepping into a spacious chamber dug out of the trash.

His Maggot flickers out as they step into the chamber, and Whack-eth cries, *"Can't you keep that thing lit? We could be stepping into a whole nest of those monsters."*

"Yeah, maybe…," Blurp concedes, squeezing his fingers around the toy's plush stomach.

As they step through the scrap, a voice calls out, *"I give it a 'B' for the best beer you ever drunk!"*

"Wahh!" Whack-eth cries. *"I just stepped on something soft."*

With a well-placed smack on the back, Blurp's Maggot flicks back on, and he shines it toward Whack-eth's feet. "It's just one of those Ol' Guard talking promotional koozies.

Don't worry, the only thing it might hurt is your ears." But upon closer inspection, he says, "This is a really old one. I bet some drunk scrapper out there would kill to get their beer in it."

"Whoa…," Whack-eth says.

Snatching the faded beer holder out of the scrap pile, Blurp tells her, "I told you coming back here would be worth it."

But when he looks to Whack-eth for some well-earned praise, she just stares up with her mouth hanging open. Bracing himself to be eaten alive, Blurp slowly lifts his Maggot to illuminate the chamber. But instead of the monster's friends, he finds its treasure — a wall-to-wall, floor-to-ceiling hoard of gently loved collectibles, promotional merchandise, and enough contraband to cause a would-be officer of the mighty Zorman fleet and citizen of the United Empires to retire early and defect to a neutral planet.

Glancing around the great collection, Whack-eth notes, *"The trash monsters are becoming disconcertingly discerning."*

For a long while, the two gaze upon the unparalleled collection in hushed awe, until Blurp finally breaks the silence to ask, "You're not going to kill me, are you?"

"What?" Whack-eth cries. *"No! Why would you think that?"*

"You could shoot me and keep all the glory and pats on the back for yourself," Blurp accuses her.

"Well, you could do that to me," she counters.

Thinking it over, he muses, "I guess I *could*, couldn't I?"

"Chut up, you chidiot," Whack-eth says. *"There's enough glory here to share with the whole academy. Of course, we won't."*

"Fish no."

"After all, while it's our duty to the United Empires to report our discovery, we also have a duty to ourselves to do it in such a way that ensures we receive all the credit."

"It's the UE way," Blurp confirms with pride.

Brow scrunching the way it does when she's in deep thought, she says, *"We have to devise a plan to get in contact with someone higher up the ranks than anybody we have access to inside the academy."*

"Well, let me know when you figure it out," Blurp says, peering up at row upon row of recycled shelves full of precious scrap.

Shining his light over the chamber, he comes across a vast assortment of neatly organized colored rectangles, and when he gets a closer look, what he discovers causes him to drop his Maggot.

"What is it?" Whack-eth asks.

Lifting his glowing toy out of the dust, Blurp glances over the tapes and says, "They're all here. This must be the most complete collection of Vulgar Videos ever assembled."

"But the UE banned those almost twenty space years ago," Whack-eth says. *"What are they doing here?"*

Carefully slipping one of the fragile objects from the shelf, Blurp squints at the back cover. "I guess the censor board dumped the confiscated tapes here, and that monster must have dragged them into its cave along with the rest of this stuff."

"You could get reprimanded just for looking at those."

"I know," Blurp says. "Isn't it great?"

"But that doesn't make any sense," Whack-eth argues. *"You're telling me that monster brought all this stuff back here for what, so it could kick back and watch some dumb horror movies in its trash museum?"*

"Hmm, that's a good point." Pressing his hands to the packed trash, Blurp searches along the wall until he finds a small switch. As soon as he flicks it, a hidden network of lights comes to dim life, illuminating the room just enough to provide a peek at the great collection surrounding them.

As Whack-eth looks around at all the scrap, she whispers, *"How the fish…"*

"Look," Blurp cries, pointing across the chamber. "There's a TV!" He follows a low hum resonating through the room over to one of half a dozen adjoining chambers and peaks inside. "It's an old generator. Looks like it runs on used ration oil." Setting his Maggot down, he lifts one of the jugs of junk oil for Whack-eth to see for herself.

"What in the fish was *that monster?"*

"Maybe it wasn't a monster at all," Blurp proposes. "Maybe it was just a lonely defector from some backspace planet we've never heard of. If we deprived it from all of this, maybe it is *we* who are the real monsters."

"But it was *a monster,"* Whack-eth says. *"I mean, it tried to eat us."*

Unable to take his eyes off the treasure trove, Blurp says, "I guess that's true."

"You guess?"

"Well, I'm not sure it was trying to eat *me*. It might have only wanted to kill me, for all I know. I'd do worse to keep greedy space pirates from getting their hands on a collection like this."

"What are you doing now?" Whack-eth demands.

Rummaging through his bag, Blurp pulls out his black gold detector and grins. "What better place to look?"

Whack-eth groans disapproval. *"Instead of hunting for imaginary moon treasure, we should be figuring out what to do with the real treasure that's all around us."*

Ignoring his space pal's command, Blurp turns the dial, and the machine starts beeping. "Huh…"

"What? What does that mean?"

Blurp shrugs and suggests, "Black gold?"

"It can't be black gold," Whack-eth cries. *"Black gold isn't real!"*

"This beauty has never led me wrong," he says, patting his trusty detector.

"It's never led you anywhere!"

"Nevertheless."

"This is insane," Whack-eth says as she paces around the scrap. *"Forget about the black gold. We've already got more treasure than we can handle."*

"Pfff," Blurp scoffs. "All this stuff combined isn't worth a fragment of a scrap of the black gold. Plus, if we discover the black gold, we won't just be heroes in the UE. We'll be heroes across the entire universe. We'll be able to do anything we want."

"But what'll we do then?"

"We'll worry about that later," Blurp decides. "For now, let's focus on finding the black gold. It's not like this stuff is going anywhere."

Nodding resolutely, Whack-eth announces, *"As leader of this expedition, I decree that we search for the black gold."*

"Well ordered," Blurp says. But as he makes to leave, he stops for one more longing gaze at the forbidden tapes and decides, "I'll just grab *C.H.U.D.*"

As soon as he pulls the tape off the wall, the garbage pile begins to quake all around them, and Whack-eth cries, *"What the fish did you do?!"*

"It must have been a load-bearing tape!" Blurp says as the walls begin to crumble, dropping big heaps of trash into the chamber below.

"We have to get out of here before this whole place collapses!" Whack-eth howls.

An old Xpresso can falls from the ceiling and bonks Blurp on the helmet, prompting him to dazedly gape at the soon-to-be once again lost treasure hoard. "But all this *stuff*. We can't just leave it here to be buried."

"Would you rather have your life or your treasure?" Whack-eth asks. *"Because you can't have both."*

Blurp mentally wishes the collection a sad farewell as Whack-eth drags him back into the trash tunnel just before the chamber crashes down. Trudging through the scrap as fast as their spacesuits can cut the thin atmosphere, they soon find themselves in a familiar section of tunnel, where the walls are coated in monster blood. As Blurp plods through the carnage, his foot lands in one of the dark puddles, and his legs slip out from under him, sending him crashing onto his back. Whack-eth comes around to help him up, but she loses her balance, and suddenly they're both on the ground writhing in the goop. Pawing at each other through slippery space gloves as the walls fall down around them, they somehow manage to get to their feet and cautiously shuffle their way back to the mouth of the cave.

The storm has calmed some during their expedition, and they stumble outside just in time to watch the tunnel collapse in on itself. Looking back in horror, Blurp falls to his slimy knees and quietly sobs for their loss.

"You really know how to fish up a good thing," Whack-eth laments. *"But hey, we don't need that stuff, right? We still have the black gold, which is more valuable than the whole universe combined."*

"That's right!" Blurp exclaims, awkwardly pushing himself to his feet. "It doesn't matter if we just lost the biggest collection of priceless space relics known to humanoid kind. The only thing we need to get ahead in this universe is the black gold."

"And the black gold detector…"

"Right, all we need is the black gold and the black gold detector, and my Moon Maggot," Blurp says, finally. "And C.H.U.D."

"How does it feel knowing you've condemned both of us to pointless missions poking around dangerous dump planets for the rest of our short space lives?" Whack-eth inquires.

Wiping the goop off the screen of his detector, Blurp says, "It feels fine, because that's not going to happen." But when he turns the knob, *nothing* happens.

"You broke it, didn't you?" Whack-eth gripes. *"Does your incompetence know no bounds?"*

"I didn't break it," Blurp prays. "Just give me a space second. I built this thing myself. I know how it works." Of course, that was many space years ago, and now all he can think to do is twist the knob back and forth. With the weight of their professional and financial futures pressing down on him, he finally smacks the side of the box and the screen comes back to life. "What'd I tell you?"

With a condescending shake of her head, Whack-eth tells him, *"You're lucky. I'll give you that. But I still don't believe the black gold is real."*

"Well, we're about to find out."

Blurp leads them in the direction of the blinking dot on the screen, marching around the base of the great trash pile toward a heap of twisted metal out by junk's edge. The trek is slow and annoying as they try to maintain their footing over old newspapers and vast tracts of plastoid bottles while simultaneously batting away a shower of falling scrap.

As they approach the mound of charred metal, Whack-eth suddenly asks, *"Why didn't it go off before?"*

"What, off, when?" Blurp blurts. "I think the interference in our helmets has gotten worse."

"The black gold detector," Whack-eth says, with more than a hint of aggravation. *"Why didn't it detect anything when you first tried it?"*

"Huh…" Blurp squints down at the screen and frowns. "Maybe we weren't in range?"

"But we're not far from where we were," she argues.

"It's a mystery," Blurp says. "Anyway, it must be in here somewhere. The little dot is really blinking now."

Looking out over the vast scrap pile thrown out before them, they reluctantly get their hands filthy. Blurp hefts aside an armful of what he assumes is worthless refuse before he takes a closer look at the Magic Meatball he's holding and realizes that the stuff out here is almost as good as what the monster had stashed away.

As Whack-eth prepares to launch a ratty Barbarella doll out of the atmosphere, Blurp cries, "Wait! There's a lot of good stuff here. We have to be gentle. We can't just toss it."

"Why?" she asks. *"Somebody else did. I thought we were looking for the black gold. What does it look like, anyway?"*

Shrugging, he says, "I figure we'll know it when we see it."

Even as Whack-eth roughs up the pile, Blurp retains a healthy respect for the disposed, carefully relocating once-cherished treasures while sorting out the *really* good stuff for himself. As he digs through a discarded collection of sparkly stuffed animal-like creatures, he comes upon a large hunk of jagged metal and waves Whack-eth over.

"What is it?" she asks.

"I don't know," Blurp says, motioning to all the semi-valuables covering it. "It looks big. Help me move this stuff — and try not to devalue anything, for Space God's sake."

As they clear away the scrap, Whack-eth says, *"There's something painted on the side. It's probably just some old junker somebody dumped."*

As Blurp exposes the words, he reads, "Ster-oid Jon."

"Told you."

"Who do you think that is?" he asks.

"Probably just some backspace scrap dealer who go in over his head," Whack-eth says, dismissively.

Further down in the plush pile, Blurp discovers a large hole in the ship's hull. Peeking inside, he finds the scattered remnants of Jon's living room, including a busted couch, a scorched junk table, and a smashed television set, among other artifacts.

As he squeezes down inside, he tells Whack-eth, "Watch my back, will you?"

"You're not going in there, are you?" she moans. *"It's just a crummy junker. That thing is probably crawling with dust goblins."*

Ignoring her objections, Blurp lowers himself into the ship and crash-lands in a heap of old ration trays. Once he scrambles to his feet, he uses his Moon maggot to light the cabin. Whack-eth was right — there's not much to see. Torn wires hang from the ceiling, and up in the cockpit, all the windows have been smashed in. The back half of the ship is missing entirely, replaced by a dense mass of scrap.

In the corner of the room, Blurp notices a dented mini fridge surrounded by a pool of clear liquid. Attached to the door under a magnet from some kids show, he finds a picture of a feline scrapper and some other ackle standing outside an ancient-looking moon mansion. Shrugging, he tosses the picture to the floor and rips open the little door to find a single can of Ol' Guard that miraculously survived the crash. He slips the can into his bag for later, but as he turns to leave, something else catches his eye.

He stares into the dark abyss of the broken TV, entranced by the space between its glass fangs, when he realizes there's something inside of it. Carefully reaching between the jagged teeth, he gets a hold of what he, for a moment, mistakes for the darkness itself, and he pulls out a small black cube. Its surface is so black, he almost didn't see it.

"Are you done messing around in there?" Whack-eth cuts in. *"I must have lost my mind, letting you convince me to dig through this garbage pile. I never thought anything could be worse than trash duty at The Park."*

As Blurp pulls himself out of the wreckage, he points out, "You said doody."

"Be that as it may," Whack-eth grumbles. *"I'm done wading through the chit looking for pretend treasures. As soon as we get back, I'm reporting you to the commandant for incompetence, dereliction of duty, and being a bad space pal."*

"Hey, that's not brule!" Blurp cries. "If it wasn't for me, we never would have found that monster's treasure trove."

"We also never would have destroyed it in irrecoverable fashion," she says, adding insult to insult.

"And we never would have found *this*." Angrily reaching into his bag, Blurp emerges with the black cube he found inside the old junker and presses it against Whack-eth's porthole.

"What is it?" she asks, her anger morphing into something like wonder.

Pulling the cube out of reach before his pal can get her grubby space gloves on it, Blurp says, "I think it's… black gold."

"It's not black gold," she argues. *"Black gold isn't real."*

"What else could it be?" he demands.

Whack-eth's face twists, and after a moment, she finally suggests, *"A paperweight?"*

"It's the real thing," Blurp insists. "I can feel it. And as the ancient commercials so often repeated, ain't nothing like the real thing."

"If you can feel it, it's probably melting our brains as we speak."

"It's not a physical feeling but more of a gut one."

"Oh, you mean bullchit," Whack-eth clarifies.

But as she looks more closely, she grows quiet, and for a long moment, they both bask in the cube's incredible blackness, until a crackly voice rudely interrupts their shared trance.

"Gimme that thing."

"Did you hear something?" Whack-eth asks.

"Um… no," Blurp decides.

Sensing a presence other than their own, they turn back toward the junker to find the specter of an old scrapper hovering next to them.

"I said gimme,*"* the translucent scrapper moans, its wispy form flickering in the starlight.

"G-give you what?" Blurp stammers.

"The black gold," the apparition says. *"It's a cursed object. You don't want it. Also, it belongs to* me, *not you."*

"So it really is the black gold," Blurp announces, exultant. "I told you!"

"Chut up, you chidiot!" Whack-eth says. *"This guy is going to kill us, or something. Give him the stupid cube!"*

"No way!" Blurp cries. "After everything we've been through, he's going to have to pry it from my body's soulless fingers."

"If that's what it takes," the phantom scrapper howls, lunging for the object in Blurp's hand.

Yelping at the sight of the angry old man as he swoops toward them, Blurp and Whack-eth take off tripping down the mountain of trash.

As they stumble onto the littered moonscape, the scrapper yells after them, *"Get rid of that thing while you still have the chance. You can leave it here, with me!"*

They keep running until the junker is out of earshot and then they run some more. All the while, Blurp stares at the mythical object in his hands, transfixed by its innate desirability.

"What do you think that thing was back there?" Whack-eth finally asks, still sounding spooked.

"It looked like a ghost," Blurp says.

"Ghosts aren't real!"

"Fine, then what do you think it was?"

Shrugging, she suggests, *"Moon gas?"*

Shifting his attention back to the object in hand, Blurp says, "Who cares? Whatever it was, it confirmed that this is the real black gold. I can't wait to see the look on the commandant's warped face when he finds out I'm one of the richest citizens in the UE."

"Don't get ahead of yourself," Whack-eth warns. *"If it turns out to be a fake, we'll just be proving our own incompetence, while simultaneously undermining faith in the institutions which we hold so dear. Assuming the old coot knows what he's talking about, and that's the assumption of a lifetime, then we have to figure out how we're going to report this."*

"Uh, right, report…"

"Though incredibly unlikely, we have to plan for even the most improbable of eventualities," she says. *"If that cube is, in fact, the black gold, then everyone in the academy is going to try to take credit for its discovery. We have to ensure that we remain an integral part of whatever 'official' story they cook up."*

"I say we keep it for ourselves," Blurp suggests. "Why share it with all those ackles?"

"You think they're just going to let us keep it?" Whack-eth asks. *"We're on an official mission, dumb as it is. We won't make it past baggage check without someone finding it."*

"What if we hide it out here and come back for it when we're off-duty?"

Whack-eth stops in the middle of the scrap and says, *"I feel obliged to point out that you said doody. In spite of that faux pas, you may have finally landed on a plan that isn't completely chidiotic."*

"Thank you."

"This way, we're technically relinquishing ownership, even if only for a short space time. But if we're going to do this, we have to agree to act with the utmost discretion."

Blurp nods, pretending to understand what the fish she's talking about. "Right, utmost…"

"It means don't say chit to anyone!" Whack-eth barks. *"Don't even talk to yourself. There's always someone listening."*

That last point Blurp has come to understand all too well. Unable to recall the last time he voluntarily spoke to anyone in the academy about anything of any importance whatsoever, he says, "Consider it done."

"Good," Whack-eth says. *"We'll stash the cube someplace repellent, and the next time our schedules line up, we'll fly back out here. Once we get to the drop pod—"*

Before she can finish delivering her orders, an incoming transmission appears inside Blurp's porthole, and he cries, "Chit, chit, what do we do?"

"Chut up and stay calm," Whack-eth instructs. *"It's probably just the commandant wondering why we've been down here so long. We'll say we got stuck in the trash storm, which is mostly true. Just let me do the talking."*

But when the feed connects, Blurp is met by a face even steelier and more devoid of emotion, a feat which just space seconds ago he would have considered inconceivable. Clad in his finest black-and-white's, the UE commander regards them with a stare so piercing that Blurp figures he must be peering into their souls. He gives off the impression of a guy who would eat his own men for breakfast if he was hungry enough, and he looks starved.

When the 'Big Ear,' as the trainees at the academy have gotten accustomed to calling the invisible elites that comprise the upper-ranks of the UE, clears his throat, he does so with such force that it causes Whack-eth to stammer, *"V-Vice Admiral Zok, s-sir it's an honor t-to—"*

"You can dispense with the hero worship, appropriate though it may be," the vice admiral says. *"At ease, cadets. I want to hear about this 'black gold' you found."*

Blurp instinctively plays dumb, "Black gold?"

Staring through the feed, unblinking, the vice admiral says, *"Before either of you says something that could be construed as a lie, I will remind you that all communications within the UE are monitored, even those inside your helmets. Knowing that I have already personally reviewed every word you've uttered since you landed on that trash ball, I want you to think long and hard about the next words that come out of your mouths. They will very likely determine not only your fate, but that of the entire United Empires."*

Nervously glancing at each other through their feeds, Whack-eth announces, *"Good news, we found the black gold!"*

"That is *good news,"* the vice admiral says, the edges of his lips faintly twitching.

"And all that stuff about keeping it for ourselves was just a joke," Blurp adds.

"Don't worry," the vice admiral assures them. *"I would have thought less of you if you hadn't at least considered keeping the element for yourselves. You two have done your conglomeration of galaxies proud. If what you've discovered is the genuine object, with its presumably boundless power, it will allow us to solidify our hold over the universe! But you must tell no one — especially the commandant. He'd give his other eye to get credit for this. I want to make sure you two are properly taken care of. I will have your ship rerouted to the base for an unannounced contraband inspection, where I will meet with you personally. Do you think you can get it here in one piece?"*

Taking a cue from his space pal, Whack-eth says, *"Consider it done."*

"I will consider it done when the element is securely in my grasp," the vice admiral tells them.

"*Right…,*" she says.

The Big Ear stares at them dubiously for a long moment and finally says, "*The UE is counting on you. Don't fish it up!*"

"*You can count on—*" but the feed cuts out before she can say, "*us.*"

Left to fend for themselves amidst the falling junk, the space cadets continue their march back to the drop pod in sullen silence, until Blurp finally says, "Do we really have to give the black gold to that ackle?"

"*Ah-ha-ha,*" Whack-eth laughs mechanically. "*He's just kidding around, or not, depending on whatever is most to your liking, sir.*"

"No I'm not," Blurp argues.

"*Yes,*" Whack-eth insists, miming the universal sign for 'they're listening.' "*You are.*"

"Oh… right."

"*Anyway, this is the best thing that could have happened,*" she claims. "*We don't know what the black gold really is or if it's even real. We'd probably get ourselves killed trying to fence it. This way it's out of our hands, with us having done our duty. You heard the vice admiral. We're going to be heroes when we get back. Pretty soon we'll be at the top of the UE command chain ordering around losers like us.*"

"I guess," Blurp concedes, staring into the dark object temporarily secured between his space gloves. "I just wish I didn't have to go back to the academy. When this is all over, I'm getting the fish out of the UE. Maybe I'll move to a quiet planet somewhere, or start hanging out with the spaceheads over at The Park. Either way, it's going to be better than this."

Whack-eth stares into Blurp's helmet, and for the first time all mission, she smiles. "*That's the spirit! Once we deliver the black gold, we'll be free to do whatever we want. It's going to make all our dreams come true, in a roundabout way.*"

"You really think so?" Blurp says.

"Does time fly when you're having fun?"

"Uh…"

"The answer is yes," Whack-eth says. *"Don't you know anything? It was formally proven centuries ago by the famous space pirate, Ponce Raleigh."*

"Oh," Blurp says. "Well… brule!"

Having come out ahead for a change, they smack their gloves together, triumphantly, like true space pals.

With the worst of the trash storm behind them, the last leg of their journey is a piece of ration cake. Before long, they reach the drop pod, and as Blurp wrenches the door open, he spots a faint glimmer on the horizon.

Zooming in through his porthole, he tells Whack-eth, "Looks like a Traxan warship."

"Huh," she muses. *"I wonder what they're after."*

About the Author

Andrew Bixler materialized just a short-ish drive from the same interdimensional crossroads as Bootsy, baby! He writes fiction that'll funk you up. He is also co-host of Big Orange Couch: The 90s Nickelodeon Podcast.

For more about the author, news about upcoming books, and contact information, visit andrewbixler.com

For more about the Big Orange Couch podcast, visit bigorangecouch.podbean.com

Thanks for Reading

I am grateful that you chose to spend your hard-earned crits on my book. If you enjoyed this book, please spread the word to every sci-fi adventure fan you know. The fate of my world depends on it!

How Was the Ride?

If you've come this far, maybe you're willing to come a little further. I am an independent author, and I can use all the feedback I can get. Let me know what you think of this book by leaving a review on Amazon, Goodreads, or by shooting me a message!